EVERY FRIDAY

DAN YACCARINO

Henry Holt and Company

New York

Henry Holt and Company, LLC
Publishers since 1866
175 Fifth Avenue
New York, New York 10010
www.henryholtchildrensbooks.com

Library of Congress Cataloging-in-Publication Data
Yaccarino, Dan.
Every Friday / Dan Yaccarino.—1st ed.
p.   cm.
Summary: Every Friday a father and his child share a special ritual.
ISBN-13: 978-0-8050-7724-7
ISBN-10: 0-8050-7724-3
[1. Father and child—Fiction. 2. City and town life—Fiction.] I. Title.
PZ7.Y125Eve 2007   [E]—dc22   2005020253

First Edition—2007 / Book designed by Dan Yaccarino and Donna Mark
The artist used gouache on watercolor paper to create the illustrations for this book.
Printed in the United States of America on acid-free paper. ∞

1   3   5   7   9   10   8   6   4   2

AUTHOR'S NOTE

Every Friday, my son, Michael, and I have breakfast together
at the corner diner. Since he turned three, this has been
our special time together and our favorite day of the week.
I hope that you, too, will start a little tradition like ours.

Friday is my favorite day.

Every Friday, Dad and I leave the house early.

Even if it is cold,

snowing,

sunny,

or raining.

We see the shops open.

And the building on the corner going up bit by bit.

We look at lots of things along the way.

We get friendly waves,

Everyone is rushing, but we're taking our time.

"Three more blocks to go," says Dad.

and we give them right back.

We count the dogs,

and I mail our letters with a little help.

"C'mon," I say.

"Only one more block to go."

At last—breakfast at the diner!

"Let me guess," Rosa the waitress says.
"Pancakes, right?"

We look out the window
and watch people hurry by.

While we eat, Dad and I talk about

all sorts of things.

But soon it's time for us to go.

Already, I can't wait.